THE DAY BEFORE CHRISTMAS

A Story of Charlotte and Emilio

by Barbara Westman

Harper & Row, Publishers

The Day Before Christmas   Copyright © 1990 by Barbara Westman
Printed in the U.S.A. All rights reserved. 1   2   3   4   5   6   7   8   9   10   First Edition

Library of Congress Cataloging-in-Publication Data
Westman, Barbara.
   The day before Christmas : a story of Charlotte and Emilio / by Barbara Westman.
      p.   cm.
   Summary: Young dogs Charlotte and Emilio spend Christmas Eve playing in the snow,
wrapping presents, trimming the tree, and going for a sleigh ride.
   ISBN 0-06-026428-4 : $ — ISBN 0-06-026429-2 (lib. bdg.) :
$
   [1. Christmas—Fiction.   2. Dogs—Fiction.]   I. Title.
PZ7.W52625Day   1990   89-29424
[E]—dc20   CIP
                                                                        AC

For Laura Geringer, Christine Kettner,
Arthur Danto, and Charlotte and Emilio too,
of course.
And for all my friends.

B. W.

On the day before Christmas, it is snowing.

Charlotte and Emilio have cocoa for breakfast. Emilio makes a mess.

They help their mother clean house. Watch out, Emilio!

There is so much to do before Christmas.

Later they help their next-door neighbors, the twins, dig out the snow. Charlotte does all the work while Emilio plays.

The twins ask them in to bake cookies.
Delicious!

Time out for skating with their friends.

On their way home, they stop at the toy store.

It's starting to get dark.

Charlotte and Emilio rush to wrap their presents. It's easy to tell which ones Emilio wrapped.

Their father drives them to Treeland.
There are so many trees, it's hard to
choose—but Emilio knows exactly which one
he wants.

Back home, they trim the tree.
Emilio hangs up his stocking for Santa.

After supper, they sing Christmas carols in the cold.

Charlotte has a pretty voice. Emilio just likes to sing.

The twins invite everyone in for cookies.
Emilio feels so happy, he does a handstand.

Charlotte and Emilio take a sleigh ride home.

It has stopped snowing, and everything is quiet. In the distance, Charlotte thinks she hears a faint tinkling of bells.

Good night, Charlotte.
Good night, Emilio.
Merry Christmas.

FOR SANTA